Love Me for Who I Am

By Sonya Visor

Tru U Books

Covenant House Press

Real ♥ Raw ♥ Risqué ♥ Inspirational Books

Love Me for Who I Am

©2014, 2017 by Sonya Visor

Covenant House Press\TruU Books, LLC
Racine, WI 53408
covenanthousepress@yahoo.com
truubooks@gmail.com
Copyright © 2014 by Sonya Visor
ISBN -10:0-9843541-3-1
ISBN -13:978-0-9843541-3-9
Library of Congress Control Number: 2014920560
Published in the United States of America
Original Published Date: December, 2014

Cover Artist: Melissa Talbot
www.itsmelissatablot.com

Interior Design: Susan Harring
harring87@att.net

Books by Sonya Visor

Inspirational

Who I've Become

I'm Coming Out, With My Hands Held-Up High

(Forthcoming Title)

Non-Fiction Anthologies

Love. Hope. Faith *(Who Shall Save Me From Myself)*

SistahFaith *(My Own Creation)*

Blended Families (The Check for $3.96)

Fiction

Love Me For Who I Am - a novella

Got to Be Real *(Forthcoming title)*

Make It Last Forever *(Forthcoming title)*

Let's Drink To That *(Forthcoming title)*

Fiction Anthologies

All I Want For Christmas *(Unwrap the Gift)*

A Time of Praise: Christmas Anthology *(Giving You the Best of My Love)*

When She Loves *(Taken)*

Dedication

This book is an offering unto the Lord God Almighty.
The Love of God can pick you up if you want to be lifted.
I know…because it *lifted* me. God's Love is a gift.

1 Peter 4:8: Above all, love each other deeply,
because love **covers** over a multitude of sins

TABLE OF CONTENTS

CHAPTER 1

I stared out the window, captivated by the movie replaying in my mind. I saw myself anticipating each delicate kiss, and the strong, tender embrace of his arms. Each caress forever engraved on my mind. I was trapped in a cycle of addiction because of what I had enjoyed.

"Whew, it's getting hot in here," I sat, fanning myself with my hand.

A few months had passed since our encounter, but the fire from those images of Malik and me still burned extra hot. My mother's house should have been the safest place to meet Malik. I'd never be sinful *inside* Mama's house. But I was wrong to lie to myself with my hormones raging.

Our earlier phone conversation and the text messages already had me simmering. I had no business meeting up with him. My burner had grown from warm to hot. As soon as he grabbed me from behind and wrapped his arms tight around me, pulling me close, I cupped my hands into his and held on. I felt the warmth of Malik's breath as his lips brushed against my neck. My mind told me to cherish this moment in his arms. But I rebelled and turned to face him. I kissed him like he was going off to war.

And we ended up in Mama's bed.

It was so good.

I had it bad.

Malik wasn't my first lover, but he held the title of being my best. Every time I tried to refocus my mind, my thoughts snapped back like a rubber band to his sexier than legal body. I tried to suppress the tantalizing images, but I was in a prison cell I didn't want unlocked.

The truth was I loved how Malik made me feel.

So, I was stuck in this forbidden place. I never did any of the chasing. I just slowed my church strut down long enough to be caught in his web of sensuality. I could hear Mama saying, "*I raised you better than how you actin', Rainey Thomas.*"

At one time, Mama's voice used to be stronger than the lustful call that pulled me toward the sheets, but then I heard and answered his siren call. Since then, I tried to block out her voice.

"Rain, open up. It's me."

My oldest sister was one of only two people who knew I had a two-bedroom suite at the new Hyatt in Milwaukee. The contemporary suite, decorated with earth tones and hints of red functioned as my hideaway and escape from reality for the past week.

The king-size mattress buried beneath gold pillows was inviting, but the rest I needed wouldn't come. I'd fallen in love with the cuddly, oversized tan chaise in the mini sitting room where I sat taking in the scenic view. The snow-draped pine trees mesmerized me, creating the perfect backdrop for my instant replays of moments spent in Malik's arms.

"I'm coming. Give me just a second." I wiped my eyes and tucked my medium-length black curls behind my ear. In an attempt to look presentable, I swiped a powder puff quickly over my cheekbones. My sister's sharp discernment was akin to a human radar system, so I took another minute to smooth my pink cotton pajama top. The material mirrored my down and flannelly feelings. Usually, I'm the dress up type. Since I got the news, all I wanted to do was wrap up in a blanket and comfort myself.

Maybe Zora wouldn't notice my slightly bloodshot eyes. I gave myself a once-over in the bathroom mirror and smiled. I'd heard smiling when you look and feel crazy helps cover up what's really going on inside. I decided to give that technique a try.

I swung the door open before she could knock again. "Hey there, girl." We couldn't embrace because Zora's arms were wrapped around four brown grocery bags.

"You knew I was coming. Why did it take you so long to answer the door? Who's here?" Zora peered over my shoulder.

Ignoring Zora's questions, my attention zoomed in on the paper sacks weighing her down. I took two from her arms and led the way to the kitchen portion of the suite. I could tell from her body language she was about to set off my 'Irritate Me' alarm. Her greeting had already set my nerves on edge. People just needed to come in, say hello, and have a seat.

"I know you heard me."

I wanted to scream, *and you already know the answer*, but I held myself together and responded like I once knew Jesus in my life. I sighed. "You know I'm alone."

"Well, did you change your mind about me helping with the program at church or what?" Zora halted, setting her bags on the counter.

"I asked *you*..." I paused before adding, "Come on now. I'm just having second and third thoughts about working at the church after moving away." Zora seemed okay with my response, so I teased, "And you stopped going to the church...just like I did."

"Not quite. I stopped going to *that* church, but I do attend church. I still work with Pastor Chris, on occasion. From a distance."

"Is it because of how *fine* our pastor is?"

"No, not at all," Zora said with a wicked smile. "But he *is* something to look at."

"I bet he tempts some of those singles, and even married women, every Sunday morning."

We shared a laugh and high-fived one another.

It was good to laugh with her. It'd been a while. At thirty-two, Zora had three years on me, so I would always be her baby sister. People often mistook us for twins. That was a compliment. We were so much alike, but she was classier and more of a rule follower.

I tried to follow the rules.

Zora was a pearl necklace type of lady, while I was more like dangling earrings. She had a flair that could change the atmosphere of any room. Standing next to Zora made me analyze myself, and I didn't like that. No woman should feel the need to compare herself to another and I wouldn't be compelled to do that if she didn't remind me so much of Mama.

"What's all of this?" I started unpacking the items as Zora went back into the hallway to grab the last few plastic grocery bags, bags from a different store filled with more treats.

"We're going to eat a few snacks while we catch up. If you want, we can order pizza," Zora suggested, "or get carry-out later while we work on the community project."

"Mmm-hmm." I shook my head. I didn't recall agreeing to work all night on anything. Zora fixed her gaze on me, and I pretended not to notice.

"A mini restaurant full of snacks *and* ordering pizza." I muttered under my breath. "What happened to your no-snack rule?"

Zora searched through the items. "This is not about me. I'm here to work and we need fuel, don't we?"

Zora surprised me when she agreed to help with the Christmas program at Mama's church. She used to avoid church as much I did when Mama passed away. I hadn't graced the steps of any church since Mama left us. And it's sad to say, but I was relieved.

I might not be the only one with a few secrets, seemed like she might have a few issues of her own. On top of that, now she was eating unhealthy and whatnot? Her focusing on her own issues is what I needed, because the last thing I wanted was for Zora to zero in on my struggles.

I peeked into each paper bag. One grocery bag held barbeque and regular potato chips. Another contained chocolate chip cookies. After finding the large jar of peanuts, I couldn't plow through the bags anymore. My stomach zigzagged with each new food. I noted the goodies, thankful for the distraction. It had been a few minutes since I thought of Malik.

With one hand on my stomach, I admitted, "I can't eat right now," and walked away.

"I got some of your faves." Zora smiled as she scanned the banquet of snack foods.

I hated how well she knew me. Cookies and chips were almost as addicting as Malik.

Ugh. I needed to stop thinking about that man. I smiled. "A little later, sis."

Zora offered me a cookie anyway. I tried to muster enthusiasm for the treat while struggling to stabilize my stomach. Not an easy task to do while undercover.

Zora placed a cheese tray, some finger sandwiches, and what looked like a small pound cake on the black desk. Then, she peered at me and said, "Now, what's really going on? You're smiling, but I'm not feeling it."

I waltzed back over by the spread of goodies and whipped open the bag of barbeque chips I really didn't want. Not seeing any bowls, I avoided eye contact with my sister and fixed a small serving for myself on a paper towel. I placed a single chip in my mouth and held it there so I didn't have to talk. If I were still a praying woman, I would have asked God to not let these chips set my tummy off. He must've heard my thoughts because after the first chip melted, I confidently popped another one in my mouth.

"You heard me, Rainey Thomas. What's going on?"

"What? You know how it is. The best thing for me is to stay far away from all those church folks." I tugged at my earlobe, then muttered, "...and him."

"Don't speak lies," Zora snapped, wagging a finger in my face. "It's more than that and you know it. One day you are going to get enough of trying to ride out life's storms by yourself. You always calling me after you're in too deep."

"What?" I grimaced. "I mean, um, what are you talking about?"

She stared me down with one eyebrow cocked.

Exasperated, I threw my hands in the air. "You'd never get it anyway."

"I hoped my sister would have the decency to tell me the truth. Why do I have to hear about you from those critical people down at the church?" Zora's expressive hands finally landed on her hips. "Are you really acting like you don't know what I'm saying here?"

"If you already know, why bother coming in here with all your nosy questions?" I wasn't about to fill out a questionnaire. Zora's Mother Thomas-self could take several seats. "It's nothing I can't handle." I shrugged.

Wait a second. What was Zora doing at Mama's church if she's been attending somewhere else?

Before I had a chance to ask, she continued. "Apparently, you insist on lying to me when there are drug addicts looking for you. Thomas girls are better than this, Rain. You know Mama wouldn't—"

"Don't bring Mama into this. I can't take that right now." I grabbed a pillow and held it to my tummy for support, not that it would calm the upside-down position my insides were trying to take, but it gave me something to do with my hands.

"You can't take what? Mama's ways were strict, but—"

"But nothing," I said with a raised voice. "Between Mama's perfectionism and *yours,* I can't win." I slapped my palm against my mouth and splayed my fingers. "I'm sorry, sis." After a regretful sigh, I added, "I didn't mean it like that."

"Sure you didn't, Rain. I'll be in the bedroom putting my things away." Zora marched into the unused bedroom and I landed in front of the living room window.

Silence filled the air.

I didn't know who I feared most, God or my deceased mother. Wasn't that something? You had to know my mother to know what I meant. After all, church folks didn't call my mother "Mother

Thomas" because of her age. Honor was given to her because she demonstrated God's love in her work for the Lord. Mama's wisdom earned her that title. You could write the word "Bible" across her chest in capital letters. She was a walking epistle. I could hear her even from the grave.

"I hate to even go on over to the church seein' them women's over there makin' themselves look like Jezebels, chasing the reverend right up in the church. I'm so glad I didn't raise my girls like them hot church gals. No, not my girls. They are keeping their honey to catch them some good ol' saved men."

I was raised by a single mother with principles. She always said what's in the heart will eventually come out if it's not dealt with. If I were mad at anyone, it was me I despised.

The way I had ripped into my sister shocked me. The horrified look on Zora's face told me I'd overdone it. It seemed like I was always hurting somebody since Mama died, but I wasn't one of those people who took things out on others, especially my sisters. I was just far from God and I knew it. My body ruled everything in my life lately and I didn't like it. I hated being weak. At the same time, I didn't know how to stop what I had allowed to creep into my life, my heart, and my bed.

Make that Mama's bed, his bed… *Lord Jesus, help me.*

Who would have thought things would get this out of hand? But I knew exactly how I had arrived in this miserable place. I was a strong black woman who knew the rules of engagement. Living under the "goody two-shoes" curse for many years, I showed people my best behavior while covering up all my minor infractions. The power Malik held over me defied explanation.

I broke the awkward silence, walking over to my sister. "I'm sorry. I haven't been myself, Zora, but that's not your problem."

"Okay, let's clear the air for real." Zora inched closer to me, shooting words at me like she held a loaded gun. "Do the words *murderer* and *drugs* turn on the light for you?"

"Put the darts down. No gimmicks and please, speak English," I retorted.

"You know what I'm talking about, Rain. Stop playing." Zora sauntered over to the makeshift buffet and picked up a few cheddar cheese cubes and crackers. Clearly, I wasn't the only one off her game today. Zora never snacked aimlessly. Her slender figure attested to that.

"I'm not playing with you. I just don't feel like being questioned right now about drugs or Malik," I answered. Besides, now I was suspicious as to what was going on with her.

"Are you sleeping with him?" She stared me down.

No, she didn't. Zora had a lot of nerve. I looked to the heavens and asked myself how was this any of her business? I paced to avoid answering, then plopped back down in the chair.

"Well, I guess I have my answer." Zora shook her head and clucked her tongue. Humph.

"Yes, Ms. Nosy, I've been with him in that way. So?" I placed my hand on my hip, daring her to continue.

We held each other's gazes until she broke eye contact and said, through tight lips, "Oh, so this is what you do? Stand here and disrespect me?"

"Disrespect you? You are not Mama, Zora. So stop acting like her." I did that thing where my neck roll matched my tone and then clapped out these last words, "Get your own life." *Whew, Lord.*

Zora rolled her eyes and continued, "Then it's true about the drugs and the dirty money because you're dealing with *the* Malik Johnson, the one with the—"

"You're not going to stop, are you?" I crossed my legs and folded my arms as I watched her scroll through her phone.

"Well, answer my question," Zora looked up and gestured with her hand, urging me to respond.

I started to answer her when suddenly there was a knock at the door.

Zora and I suspended our conversation and stared at the door.

Who could be knocking? Malik didn't have my location, which was good. I'd probably buckle after settling my eyes on his chest.

No, I wouldn't. I'd be strong. I could be strong.

If it were Pastor Chris, he was too close to Jesus for me to converse with him—that was a no go. Anybody else standing on the other side of that door had no chance of getting in. Not today. The door would remain bolted…and unanswered.

CHAPTER 2

T he knocking persisted.

"You let somebody follow you here," I whispered, squatting as if the intruder could see inside the luxurious suite.

"Hey, I was careful. No one followed me." Zora placed her hand on her chest and glanced back at the door with wide eyes.

"I'm not leaving, so open up!" a female's forceful voice demanded through the closed door.

"Tory!" Both Zora and I yelled her name, and then smiled at each other with relief. We hustled to open the door before her sassy tail made a scene in the hall. The last thing I needed was Tory screaming my name. I was supposed to be hiding from the world, not announcing my presence.

"Yeah, it's me. Rain, open this door before I—"

Zora ripped the door opened and snatched Tory by the sleeve, pulling her inside so forcefully she almost tripped. I would have laughed if I hadn't been so annoyed at her for yelling my name.

"Girl, what are you doing here? How did you find me...us?" I snapped.

Before closing the door, Zora surveyed the hallway like a security guard looking to eliminate any more surprises. God bless her for thinking about my safety.

"I've got my ways. But, unh-unh, y'all two will be the ones answering questions, not me. I'm the one with the 4-1-1." Acting like she had the upper hand, Tory pointed back and forth between us as she pushed past us to the snack bar and swiped a snack. Chomping on her chocolate chip cookie, she sashayed over to the sofa bed.

"How did Zora get a call and I didn't?" Tory cut her eye at Zora and jerked her neck my way. She pierced me with her gaze, clearly more upset with me than Zora.

"It's not like that Tory; you know it's not." I tried to sound as sincere as possible.

She shook her head, scrolling through her phone while eating her snack. We would feel her wrath if she waved and dismissed us. That was her signature move for "walls going up, I'm shutting you out."

The one solid thing in my life was my bond with my sisters. Zora and I were tart yet sweet together. Add our little sister, Tory to the mix and you got a spicy Hawaiian Punch. According to our mother, we were three natural beauties. Unfortunately, she held us to a standard even an angel couldn't meet. Okay, I take that back. An angel *could* meet it, but not even the holiest person on earth could measure up to Mama's expectations.

Of the three of us, Tory was the cute and sexy one, the bold one. Too bold, if you asked me.

Tory walked into church one Sunday morning wearing the shortest skirt she could find just to shame our family. She waited right until Pastor Chris was at the height of his sermon and then spread her legs. Yes, she did. And of course, he looked. What man wouldn't? Pastor Chris paused for a mere two seconds, and then continued his sermon as if nothing had happened.

Tory told us later she just wanted to see if he would take the bait. She was happy when he didn't because it proved he was a true man of God, and thus she could safely join the church. After that, she asked Pastor for forgiveness and begged him not to tell Mama. Thankfully, he never did or she might have gotten her face knocked off for that one.

"First off, how y'all gon' have a sisters' night without me?" Tory stood and folded her arms in a defensive posture. She was clearly daring us to come up with a good excuse for leaving her out.

We just put our heads down. The girl had a point, but the way I'd been feeling, I didn't know if I could handle both of my sisters at once. We knew each other too well. They eventually would have found out about my frequent bathroom hikes, not to mention tomorrow's secret appointment. For once, they didn't need to know the details. I had paid to stay in this hotel to handle my business on my own terms and that's what I planned to do.

"We're sorry," Zora apologized. "It wasn't like that."

"Mmm-hmm."

I could tell Tory wasn't satisfied as she locked eyes with me.

"What say you?" she asked.

"Sorry, baby sis. Now what's the 4-1-1?" I redirected her energy to the information I knew she couldn't wait to share.

Tory crossed her arms again, appearing agitated that she couldn't taunt us. "How come Malik is calling all our family members and acting like a fool looking for you?"

"Great," I sighed. "He must know I'm in town." I reached for my cell phone on the bed next to Tory.

Tory intercepted the phone just as the text notification rang. "He must know what?"

"Why do you insist on hiding stuff we'll find out anyway?" Zora questioned. "Is it true you are involved in his business? That's what people at Mama's church are saying. We need to know now, so we are not ambushed by these people."

I couldn't hold off any longer. I had to be a straight shooter. No more small talk.

"I need to talk to Malik first, and *then* I'll explain." The last thing I wanted to do was be short with my sister, but Zora irked me sometimes. I ran my fingers back and forth through my curls, curls I wouldn't have much longer if I kept that up, but I was troubled.

If Tory found me, it was only a matter of time before some other family member came barging in to bombard me with questions. I shifted the attention away from me. "How did you find me, Tory?"

"You didn't cover your tracks. I thought you old school girls knew how to do that, especially if you don't want Malik finding you. It won't be long before he does."

Old school girls? And Tory wondered why she couldn't hang out with us? Her twenty-two-year-old attitude always created drama.

"Stop playing, Tory," I told her.

"Okay, okay, back up. Why do I have to answer everyone else's questions, but you don't have to answer mine?" Tory extended her arms to create space so Zora wouldn't reach out and touch her. "Everybody over at the church is talking about yo' business, Rain. My question is how are you making money for this man?"

"Who is everybody?" I asked, "and give me my phone back. I see you." Tory eyed my cell phone before she handed it over, smiling at the screen. I yanked it out of her hand. "Ugh, you get on my nerves."

"I'm not the first and I won't be the last." Tory giggled, still munching on cookies.

Most of the time she could make me laugh, but today it wasn't working. I would have pulled her arms out of their sockets. Anybody who had secrets didn't want their phone handled by anyone but themselves. Scratching my head, I read a text message from Malik.

21

Meet 2nite.

I couldn't see him yet. I wasn't prepared.

"They, well, two church members in particular said Rain was up in Pastor Chris's office for a long time." Tory was telling her story in bite-sized pieces.

The two busybodies Tory spoke of, Lena and Josephine were silly middle-aged women who thought *I* wanted the pastor. They would count it a blessing to find any dirt on me because they thought I was a contender for First Lady. That was so far from reality. I enjoyed working with Pastor Chris to help bring forth the vision of hope God had laid on his heart for the ministry. That was all. More importantly, I was working hard—too hard—to cover up my drama. No way those biddies would be allowed to script the ending.

"Who are *they*? The usual bunch?" Zora asked Tory.

Tory nodded and shrugged in a nonchalant manner.

Zora turned toward me. "What were you doing in the pastor's office?"

"We had a meeting about the community Christmas program."

Zora's curiosity had heightened with the mention of Pastor Chris. She generally limited her contact with him. Mama sort of left us in his care because she esteemed him to be a godly man, even though he was a young, up and coming preacher. So, he called and checked on all of us, sometimes via email, sometimes text, but we sort of skated from under his watch, each of us drifting away. That made the most sense for Zora because she was attracted to the man, even if she wasn't ready to admit it. And it was mutual. Anyone who watched the two of them in a room could see the obvious. Looked like the good ole pastor had to ask the Lord to help him avert his eyes from Zora.

"I've got to get to him." I grabbed my coat. "Avoiding Malik was not a good idea. There's nothing worse than tenth-hand information from people who can't stand you. I have to get to Malik before those church lushes do."

Everybody knew who had the 4-1-1. Josephine and her side kick. They would do what they've done in the past with some other church nonsense; get their "friend," Malik's ex-girlfriend, Trina to stir the pot. Being a church teleprompter is how the busybodies earned their nickname — always putting words in the ears and mouths of others,

"Dressed like that?" Zora hurled her indignant question my way.

I looked down at my wardrobe. My elevator had stalled somewhere around the third floor and wasn't making its way to the top. I would never purposely run anywhere in any kind of flannels. *Get it together, Rainey Thomas.*

I head toward the clothes rack to change, but Zora and Tory blocked the way, pushing me right back down. "You're not going anywhere," Zora said.

"Especially with his crazy-nut girlfriend, Trina, lurking around asking where you are." Tory sucked her teeth. "You need to be careful. That girl is crazy and she's not letting Malik go without a fight. Don't she have a few kids by him?"

"Trina isn't Malik's girlfriend. And, he's not the father of those kids. Malik's done with her." I struggled to stand back up with the two of them towering over me. "I will talk to you all when I get back," I tried to reassure them. I searched for pacifying words, but I was distracted and in distress, an absolute no-no for me. I could not afford to crack before I finished what I had set out to do.

"Why does Trina think she has a right to be looking for you? Is this why you're hiding in a *hotel* room, to avoid controversy with Trina...Malik?"

Zora probably thought she was helping, but she wasn't.

Tory tossed the brick she'd been holding. "Do you really want to go over there now, or is it that you want to stop them from telling the whole church you were dumb enough to swirl and get pregnant by the man?"

Bam. When her words hit me, I was still standing, but everything I held fluttered to the floor. Despite my being a little removed from God, some kind of Holy Spirit must still have resided on the inside. I fixed my lips to respond, but said nothing.

As much as I loved my little sister, I couldn't believe she would disrespect me like that, not in front of Mother Thomas's replica. Text me, ask me in the bathroom, or do some kind of sign language, but do *not* blurt something like that out in front of Zora.

It wasn't what she said that hurt, because sadly, it was true. It just wasn't her place to tell *my* truth. If those long locks of hers had been a weave, my usually non-violent self would have reached over and snatched every stitched or glued-in strand out of her scalp.

24

CHAPTER 3

Tory and I held each other's gaze for what seemed like ten minutes, but probably lasted only two seconds. Stunned and embarrassed, I was exposed before my sisters. I couldn't even look at Zora who was probably in need of an oxygen tank. By the grace of God, I stayed on my feet. I shifted my weight and fixed my eyes on the beige carpet, and then looked up.

"You mean it's true?" Tory inched toward me with a questioning look in her eyes.

My heart raced. I wanted to warn her to not come any closer, but I didn't trust myself to speak.

"Is. It. True?" Tory rarely raised her voice when she spoke to me.

Me.

I shot her a "don't play with me look" as I searched to see what TV show she had tuned into this time, *I Love Lucy* or a Lifetime movie. Tory could slide from laughing to serious without warning. I glimpsed at her. By her disturbed expression, I realized she *didn't* know. I dropped my guard and answered with a simple, "Yes."

"You mean to tell me I defended you before those heifers and you…" Tory gave me her signature "whatever" wave, dismissing me from her presence. She put one hand to the back of her head and paced back and forth, scrolling through her phone with her other hand, another indicator she was done with the whole thing.

"Wait. You mean you've been out here having unprotected sex like some loose woman? At least be responsible." Zora had finally found her voice. She *would* say something like that, showing her lack of understanding, mercy, and grace. How was she able to reach sinners when she couldn't even help her own sister?

How else do you get pregnant? Shame from having my sin find me out made my face burn despite my desire to look like I had it together.

"Don't go there, Zora. Rain's not *no* loose woman. You can *stop* that."

Tory was defending me?

I looked over at her and smiled, relieved. She was the one sister I needed in my corner. We had a pact. Our secrets would never be revealed. We had the "to-the-grave" mentality. We were a safe place for one another, and I didn't want to ruin our bond. I owned my mistake and mouthed, "I'm sorry."

She nodded and winked. At least one sister was guarding my back.

"You hush up, Tory. This is the kind of thing I'd expect—" Zora abruptly closed her mouth, her accusation incomplete, but clear.

"I know what you were going to say, Zora, and that's alright. I already know what you think about me. The truth is, I'm *real* with mines and that's why I don't deal with church folks. I don't care if they're in the family or not."

Whenever Tory went into defense mode, she came out swinging with her gangster talk, which she generally reserved for the ratchet church people. Zora threw her hands up at Tory, but regret for what she had said filled her eyes.

My phone beeped again, another notification from Malik. I was about to respond when Zora snatched the phone. "Who's Teddy Bear?"

"I know it's been some years since you have kept company with a man, but I know you ain't that stupid." Tory grabbed another chocolate chip cookie, her free hand landing on her hip.

All the emotions in the last twenty minutes were stirring my appetite. Still, I couldn't eat anything just yet. The last thing I needed now was for my tummy to show its newfound power.

Zora wouldn't be satisfied until she knew my entire story. With our reputation now tainted by my carelessness, I owed my sisters an explanation. I knew my family wanted to point a gun at Malik, the drug pusher and blame him, but they couldn't. Not this time. The man had my heart and my body, which I freely gave.

Lord, why didn't I listen to you?

The mere thought of Malik caused me to shiver. I needed to put myself on a two-day fast or something. It wasn't just that he was handsome. He was as raw and real as they get. Thinking of him overwhelmed me and that wasn't good, at least not for someone with my upbringing. I could never bring him home to my family. He had issues, but who doesn't have a problem or three?

I could feel his embrace, which always quieted my mother's voice and, unfortunately, also blocked the voice of God. My mind replayed the tug-a-war until I heard Zora scream, "Talk, now!"

"Tell her the rest, Rain." Tory encouraged me with a nod. "Just tell her…so we can get on with our lives."

Indeed, my little sister did know something, either through the church or her street connections. Which group had informed her was what I wanted to know. It always amazed me how Tory could be such a great family news reporter—with everything but my stuff. Until now, our pact kept her lips shut. However, with my current news, I didn't know if she would be able to keep the lid on tight. I hoped so, because between the two of us, our secrets could be labeled scandalous.

"Who are you, Prophet Tory? I don't have time for this." I picked up my purse from the coffee table, with an exit plan to grab my clothes and coat off the hangers in the closet. I had to get to the man who needed to hear from me personally about what was happening.

"Okay, enough," Zora mumbled, raising her hands in exasperation. "I find out in a hotel room, of all places, that my sister has been lying to me?"

Inwardly, I moved toward the door, but my body remained rooted where I stood. Guilt bombarded me. Facing Zora was like facing Mama all over again. I'd rather take the truth with me six feet under than utter the words. I was normally Tory's rescuer, but this time, I was the one in need of deliverance. No matter how I looked at it, I'd lost their respect.

Outsiders had crowned the wrong sister. People thought I was the mirror image of Mama, but I was never the one. It was all a front. I didn't want to measure up to my mother—never did. That level of saintliness was too much for anyone to bear.

What I really wanted was to be free, free to make mistakes and to live without existing in the shadow of a legend. The raw reality of this sin made me tired of pretending. I wasn't perfect, but others spoke of me as if I were. My sins equaled more than three times that of Judas, and to think it all started out so innocently—at the church.

"I'm done with you because after all the times you covered me, you didn't think I'd be there for you," Zora chided.

Was she here for a scolding or to actually support me? What did she want me to say? What was there to talk about? I was pregnant. Did she want me to tell her the location, date and details of the conception?

I remained close-mouthed.

"It can't be that bad," Zora whined.

This was so not her.

"It must have been real *good*," Tory mumbled, still munching on her snacks, carelessly swinging her legs back and forth along the side of the bed.

I rushed over to Tory with my hand up like I was going to spank her, just like I did when she was little. I wasn't really going to hit her. I intended to cover her mouth to keep her quiet. I didn't know how much she knew, but the rest should come from me.

Tory wiggled away from me and bounced off the bed, placing her plate down on the table and brushing the crumbs from her hands. "Let me help you out, Sis. You are not used to living in sin and whatnot, so let me be your voice. You are an undercover freak. Now there, don't you feel better?"

While Zora's mouth gaped, I determined to finish what Tory had started, even though she was being stupid.

"Alright! Since hearing I'm pregnant is not enough, here are the horrid, spicy details you came here for." Their eerie silence caused me to hesitate a moment, but I shook it off and continued as I pointed at both Tory and Zora. "I did exactly what your mother told *me*, *you*, and *you* not to do. I slept with him, Malik Johnson, the drug lord. Not once, not twice, but repeatedly. I had sex. S-e-x."

Zora's mouth opened again, and then closed sharply.

So they wouldn't think I was one of those "fell for a bad boy" victims, I finished by saying, "And you know what?"

Knowing the question was rhetorical, neither sister answered. I studied them. I didn't know if what I saw in their faces was disappointment, disgust, or shame. For once, I didn't care.

I repeated, "And you know what?"

Neither sister looked at me as the air tightened around us. I spat out, "I enjoyed it. Every bit of the pleasure. I can't lie about it or Christianize it. I enjoyed sex with a man who's not my husband, and I didn't feel too bad about doing it…until now. Isn't that something?"

I startled myself because I had reached another dangerous place. I didn't feel that bad. In fact, I barely felt bad at all. If I weren't careful, my boisterous admission might turn into a dreaded downfall rather than the cleansing it should be. My conscience wasn't so far out the gate. I knew God would only keep me if I wanted to be kept.

If only I hadn't allowed those initial caresses…

Who was I kidding? My desire for my man's touch started well before that. It seemed as if the scriptures I'd read over the years couldn't extinguish the fiery lure. I knew better and had been ashamed to admit to myself that I hadn't wanted that flame to go out. In keeping it lit, I said no to Jesus, my mother, and the church, choosing instead to partner with sin.

Now my life was tangled and kinked up with all sorts of knots, which threatened to block me from my true destiny. I knew this wasn't it.

"What are you bragging about?" Zora's hand movements followed each word to slap her point my way. "Sexing some—" She abruptly paused, stifling her loud voice. Except for the fact that anybody on the third floor of the hotel could have heard her, she remained somewhat composed.

"See, that's why I didn't want to say anything," I blurted and turned away.

"Being pregnant is not the issue, Rain. But standing here *boasting* about what you've done, savoring it...*that* is the crisis." Zora enunciated her words more than usual.

"Everybody can't be perf—"

"Are you that naive to think you are the only one tempted to play in the devil's bed? Do you think you are so special you can stand here and glorify your sin, screaming about how much you enjoyed it? Have I failed you so much as a sister that you wish to distance yourself from the two people who will have your back when the devil is done using you?"

Tory just shook her head.

"There it is...the Mother Thomas speech," I grumbled.

Tory gasped as she grabbed Zora's wrist just inches from my face. Zora's gaze pierced me like the sun on a glass of ice on a summer day. I was about to lash out at her, but then I saw her expression, and tears crashed through my guarded wall.

I yielded the floor to her, the kind of respect you'd give a mother.

"Stop it, Rain. You are not going to guilt me about who I am. In fact, you apparently have no idea who I am because if you did, you would know I would have helped you through this, not judged you."

"But that's exactly what you're doing!" I retorted.

Zora sat down at the desk and placed her hands over her eyes. I knew she felt betrayed. Her sister, her confidant, didn't trust her enough to be honest. On top of that, I'd given voice to Zora's biggest fear. She swore she never wanted to turn into Mama. We all loved Mama, but we needed to break free from her pressure. Maybe now was the time.

My sisters left me to my sorrow after my uncut display of emotions. Unexpectedly, I felt God near and proceeded to commune with Him. The waters, which had been stopped up, escaped. No more pushing the ignore button I used all too often, especially as of late. Thankfully, there still was more Jesus inside of me than I knew.

As I sobbed, all the things I had suppressed came up and out. "I didn't mean to glorify my sins. I'm just so mad at myself. I've counseled so many teenagers and here I—"

"Rain, I'm here for you. You could have told me, of all people. Girlfriend, you know all my dirt," Tory reminded me. She had turned somber from the moment I tore the lid off my secret life, probably happy, relieved even, to know her "perfect" sisters had unspoken flaws.

"I appreciate hearing that, Tory. I'm sorry." The weeping started again. The first round of tears had been for me. This second stirring came from true repentance. Confessing my sins now freed my soul.

"After all you and I have shared, I couldn't bring myself to tell you. I was ashamed to end up *here*."

"Please, you're saving my life right now." Tory wiped her eyes before embracing me.

"I-I'm saving your life?" I questioned.

"Yes, you are. I could really do this Christian thing, but I need some non-fakers around me. True peeps. Ones who will keep me accountable. Don't take this the wrong way, sis, but you tried to anchor the world on your shoulders, and when you got tired, you gave in to everything that was pulling at you. That's why you wallowed so long."

Zora added, "She's right, you know. Whenever we asked if you were all right, you responded with—"

"I'm fine," the three of us said in unison before sharing a hearty, sniffling laugh. Zora did the same thing, so I don't know how she could cosign with Tory, but it was good to see her smile.

Zora cleared her throat and said, "Forgive me for wanting to lay hands on you. Let me join in this accountability deal. I have feelings for—"

Like a duet, Tory and I chimed out, "Pastor Chris."

"You're in love with a good, good man." Tory had learned a few lessons, but allowing others to speak for themselves was an area in which she still needed work.

Zora was clearly taken aback. "Shhh…" She placed her forefinger to her mouth and signaled for us to lower our voices, but we spoke the truth. Maybe she wasn't in love, but she sure was fond of Pastor Christopher Dockery.

Zora stared at us in contemplation. My eyes drifted to her overnight bag and briefcase. I watched as she pulled out three neutral-colored letters and handed two of them to us in a big sister manner. "These letters are from our mother, given to me by Aunt Cynthia."

Aunt Cynthia was our mother's sister and our favorite aunt. She was always there for us, and we all had a special bond with her, especially me. I received a text message from Aunt Cynthia daily. The same time every day she sent a new blessing for the day, words of encouragement. Shoot, I could make an alarm out of the chime.

Zora shared, "It's time for us to step into our own lives. Mama left instructions for me to hand these letters out at a turning point in our lives. If this isn't a turning point, what is? Now is the time."

Tory looked as if somebody had snatched the blankets off us in the dark and beamed a flashlight into our faces. I'm sure I did too.

Silently, we each took our envelope and held onto it for a few minutes. We each had a personal message from our mother. Priceless and powerful.

CHAPTER 4

I had been about to dash out of here to find Malik. I still didn't want him to hear the news from anyone other than me, but... This was a letter from Mama, a letter she wrote just for me. Even though part of me was afraid of being crucified because of Mama's walk with God, I knew she loved me. I had to stop and deal with her written words. On the one hand, I knew I was allowing Mama to continue to control me from the grave, but I needed to hear her voice, needed to know what she had to say. Malik would have to wait. I only hoped those church biddies were stopped in their tracks like Pharaoh's army was by the closing of the Red Sea.

We each found a comfortable place to sit. My suite was spacious enough to accommodate the privacy we sought. Receiving these letters tapped into the little girls within us. I began reading slowly. I wasn't two paragraphs into the letter before I could barely see through my tears.

The remembrance of my mother and all she stood for ministered to me. For once, I was receptive of her memory, free of irritations and hidden resentments.

Mama spoke from the grave, as if she were standing here talking to each of us in living color. The letters contained what we each needed to hear. I could tell because what I was feeling was written all over Tory and Zora's faces.

In my letter, Mama confessed her mistakes and her failures. She wanted her daughters to be free. She reminded me Jesus loved me and He was my rod and my shield. Her words vibrated within my soul, breaking the chains that had weighed on my neck. Like shackles falling to the ground, my strongholds crashed and crumbled around me.

"How did Mama...? I mean..." For some reason, I couldn't continue. I rocked back and forth, clutching the letter like the precious note from Heaven it was.

"This was definitely the right time." Tory looked humbled, beaming from her own fountain of joy.

Zora sat silently like she was praying. She had carried Mama's burdens since she was a teenager. Hopefully, Mama's letter released her too. She deserved some comfort and grace.

I was sure we'd share our notes with each other later, after time allowed our thoughts to settle.

"Rain, you need to cancel your appointment," said Zora in a matter of fact tone.

"What appoint—" Oh, that's right. I actually had two appointments tomorrow. One was with Pastor Chris regarding the community program and the other…

I lifted my head, looked at Zora, then glanced over at Tory, my mouth agape. Another skeleton tumbled out of the closet into the presence of my family. "How did you know?"

"Guess?" Zora smiled with a knowing look.

"Wait a minute. You mean *you?*" Tory was at a loss for words as she looked from Zora to me and then down at my stomach. She appeared softer, more vulnerable.

I nodded. What they assumed was true. I *was* the typical church girl pregnant by a bad boy. Since I wasn't too far along, I had tried to convince myself it wasn't really a baby yet. I had decided I was too old for this kind of nonsense and would rid myself of the evidence of my sin.

"Don't do it, Rain." Tory knelt before me and Zora joined her. Zora didn't say a word, but her eyes pleaded with me to not go through with the abortion. Until that moment, I hadn't seen my baby. I only saw my sin, another stain on my Christian cloth.

Tory was the first to break away from the trance we all seemed to be in. She paced in a semi-circle, as if she didn't know what to do next. For lack of a better move, she returned to her feast of goodies. I got up to join her, but halted when Tory said, "Wait a minute. Is that blood?" Frantic, she jumped up and rushed into the black and white-tiled bathroom to retrieve some towels.

"You're bleeding." Zora remained calm as she said to Tory, "Call the paramedics."

I whispered, "No, Lord, *please...*no." To Zora I said, "Call Malik for me. I need to…" My words cut off by sharp pains that hit me when I attempted to walk. I doubled over and grunted. "I'm okay. Please call him…please."

Lord, I trust you. Please forgive me and watch over this child.

Life sure was funny. Less than an hour ago, I wouldn't have even thought to pray. Tory rushed over to me with more towels. She looked frightened, but she was trying her best to remain positive. The sharp pains subsided, but I was still in agony. I expected my prayer not to be answered, but God is the Giver of life. Would He use the death of a child to teach me a lesson?

"Did you call Malik? I need to tell him." I tried to make eye contact with Zora, but she kept wrapping towels underneath me to prevent any more leakage, although I sensed no more spotting.

"You want him to come here?" Tory appeared unsure.

"Yes, because I did a horrible thing and I need to explain." I tried to maneuver onto the bed to avoid additional discomfort.

"Let us be the judge before you tell stuff that should remain buried in the sister vault," Tory advised.

All eyes were on me as I managed to get up. Thank God there was no immediate evidence of more problems, but I wanted to get to the bathroom to be sure. Midway to the bathroom, I turned toward my little sister and admitted, "I love him, Tory." In the doorway of the bathroom, I locked eyes with Zora and said with more conviction, "I *love* him."

"Well, alrighty then." Tory smiled. "But this is still sister time. Does he have to bring his tail over here right now?"

"Yes, because there's one more thing I need to rid from my soul." My hand on my stomach, I rested as I closed the door behind me. I peeked and found no evidence of any more trauma to my body. Answered prayer. *Thank you, Lord.*

"Do we need to get you to the hospital?" Zora inquired through the door.

"I think I'm good. It looked worse than it actually was." When I opened the door, Tory and Zora were standing there blocking my exit, causing me to step backward.

"You're going to keep it, right?" Tory asked.

"We'll help you with the baby," Zora assured me.

They stood motionless, awaiting my response.

"Yes, I am. Still, it's what I've already done that I need to discuss with Malik."

Blank stares lay on Zora and Tory's faces. I could see the questions. *What is she talking about? The appointment isn't scheduled until tomorrow? Should we escort her to the hospital?*

I explained. "My downfall has always been intimacy…sex. I'm a very sensual person. It is a weakness for me."

"Hey, it's a weakness of mine too, but stop sitting over there sounding like you some trick, or in Zora's words, a harlot. You're nothin' like that." Tory tried to be my cheerleader.

I cleared my throat and blinked rapidly to dam the threatening waterfall. More tears would certainly prevent me from getting through this next phase. "Please, let me continue." I took a deep breath.

"I had been celibate for nearly three years when I met Malik. Then with all the talks, walks, dinner dates, my guard began to fall. I thought I was careful, but I let him get too close to me. Dating before Malik was never an issue for me. I didn't allow the few guys I went out with to even hold my hand or be alone with me. I knew my triggers and avoided them…until Malik. I trusted him. With him, I threw away everything I knew to be right, and to top it all off," I took another breath before continuing, "the first time…was in our mother's bed."

Zora gasped and Tory spit out her soda. I imagined their thoughts. *In Mama's bed? Is she crazy? Or just hateful?*

"I know this sounds crazy, but I allowed him to see me there at the house because I just knew I'd keep it holy at Mama's. Believe me, I found out quickly how wrong I was."

I walked over to the windowsill with my back to my sisters, peering out at the picturesque pine trees perfectly covered in snow. I knew they needed a minute to digest this confession. I turned to them and said, "I paid the price. First, I laid with him. Then, I drove the getaway car—"

"You what? Rain, you helped this man rob somebody?" Tory's palms faced up as she incredulously asked me to confirm what she thought was the worst part.

"What getaway car?" Zora walked over by the window.

I'm sure she realized I needed space. Although they thought the worst was over, they had no idea what I was about to share.

CHAPTER 5

My sisters think they are ready to hear this, so Lord, help me be honest. Jesus…

I locked my eyes on the coffee pot surrounded by four black mugs in the kitchen area. I was sure I needed something to drink, but maybe not coffee.

"Almost a year ago, I walked into a building at 8:45 a.m. for my Monday morning appointment. I vividly remember this day because it changed my life. As I opened the door of Suite 219, a drab feeling came over me. The chairs were gray, the magazine table was scratched and worn, a few ceiling tiles were missing. As much money as these people made, you'd think they could at least have fixed the ceiling.

"There were no plants or pictures, just a collection of clipboards with the pens attached on strings. The face of the woman behind the sliding gray door at the receptionist desk matched the room. She was expressionless. There was a bell with a Post-It note attached to ring for service. Thank God, I didn't have to do that because my two-inch tan heels would have done an about-face.

"The receptionist told me to take a seat, fill out the form, and sign the bottom when I was done. She even pointed to the line with the X on it. I nodded, took my sheet, and searched for a secluded seat."

I waited for my sisters to shift their weight, shoot me a zillion questions…something. But they didn't move.

"As I sat there, the Spirit of God enveloped me with an urgency to leave. In the midst of that depressing atmosphere, I still felt God's love. Isn't that something? I mean, how could I feel God in that place?"

Continuing my recap, I asked, "But you know what I did? I sat there, bouncing my nervous leg. Thinking only of myself.

"Twenty minutes later, the receptionist, with her dry voice, called my name. The woman cautiously called my name again. 'Rainey, is it?'

"Y'all, I had a chance to run. The opportunity to shut everything down was handed to me, but instead I nodded and followed as if I had a leash around my neck." I paused briefly. Tory's mouth hung open and Zora peered at me with squinted eyes. Maybe, this was too hard for her to stomach, but I couldn't stop now.

"A nurse led me into a tiny procedure room. I remember how she smiled and said it would be alright as she handed me a gown and informed me the doctor would be with me shortly. As she left me in that ice cold room, she said, 'It will all be over in a few minutes.' I felt darkness above the table.

"A couple of seconds before the doctor came in, the presence of the Lord hovered around me, and I whispered to the Lord, 'I know, I know', but I laid there on the table as the tears flowed. No one but God and Aunt Cynthia knew where I was or what I was doing.

"The doctor entered and after observing my demeanor, he proceeded quickly. He was probably afraid I would burst into tears if he asked a simple, 'Are you alright?' So, he put on his gloves and tapped my legs, his way of telling me to position myself. I followed his direction and lay there giving the doctor permission to suck the very life out of me. I cried for the baby. I cried for me—for my doomed soul—and in less than fifteen minutes, it was over."

I gulped as I again walked through the very real shadow of death.

"After I killed my baby, I stopped living for God. What use could He have for me after what I'd done?" I questioned in a loud voice, beating myself on the chest. "I consented to killing an innocent bystander. That changed my life forever. I can *never* undo what I've done. I killed my baby. I killed my baby! People *want* to have children, and I, I... I didn't have the power or the right. *I took a life that I didn't give!*"

With a snotty nose and what I'm sure were bloodshot eyes, I finally got enough nerve to look at my sisters. Both of my sisters were bent forward so I couldn't really see their faces, probably digesting what they had just heard. Why had I done it? Why would I burden them with this awful sin?

Zora spoke first, her words soft, yet firm. "*Why*, Rain? You know, you didn't have to—"

I turned away from her because she looked like she wanted to swipe everything off the table. I hesitated, but I had to be honest. "Why? Because I was scared and I was afraid of what people would think of me."

"You went to some hood clinic because of..." She sputtered. "What. People. Would. Think. All this was because of...*what people would think.*" Zora hollered at me, emphasizing those four words over and over. She had lost it. I'd never seen her this irate before.

Tory stood between us, placing her hand on Zora's chest in effort to calm her down and save me from another attempted slap. "Come on now, sis. She already feels bad enough."

Zora removed Tory's hand and drew closer to me. "You only wanted to cover up your mess. Here our mother raised us to take responsibility for our actions, and you go and cover your tracks. I can't believe you planned to do the same thing again. Why?"

Close lipped, I sat down because I knew her wrath wasn't yet expended.

"Did you feel better? Did you wash your hands after you killed?" Zora questioned before she paused.

The look on her face revealed the restraint of the Spirit. She clamped her hands to her head as if she couldn't tolerate hearing much more. "After it was over, were you relieved?"

Enough! I stood up with Tory right beside me and said, "I'm not going to answer you. Because if you had any kind of sense, you would know I felt like it should have been me."

"You will answer *every* question! You owe me that much," commanded Zora. The rational one was on an emotional roller coaster. In a manner of ten minutes, Zora had shouted, sobbed, and spewed anger and conviction as she unraveled before me. In her eyes, I'd backslid and backstabbed, ruthlessness in its highest form. Would I feel the same way if it had been her instead of me?

"It's one thing to make a mistake and another to cover up your stuff so people won't talk about you," Zora debated.

She would never comprehend or be able to wrap her brain around nonsense like this. I deserved that because I had done wrong before God.

Nobody knew how I wallowed in this deadly sin. I could never undo this treacherous deed. It was excruciating to believe I was so self-centered and vain, only considering myself, not the precious life I carried. Worse, I planned to do it all over again tomorrow by going to the clinic. My rushed thoughts of suicide were no match for the pain I knew from experience I was destined to feel again.

I attempted suicide once before by taking pills, but the grave difference between killing my baby and killing myself was my death would have been *my* choice. My baby never had a voice. I made the appointment, paid the fee, and aborted my baby. Only other women who had been there could understand the agony.

Every question others threw at me, I could toss back. "Been there, asked that," I could say. Yes, I was, and still am, a Christian. Yes, I knew my actions were preposterous, and I've never said differently. No justification would ever suffice, and nothing would bring my baby back.

The overwhelming grief finally erupted. My upper body shuddered as I conveyed my heart. "I shouldn't have taken my baby's life, but I don't owe you an apology. You are not my judge. I answer to God alone for this. I *know* I displeased God." I looked off from Zora and smoothed invisible wrinkles on my top, a nervous habit of mine. "It was awful, Zora. You hear me? I was wretched, and oh, so wrong. I have beaten myself up more than you'll ever know."

I bawled so loudly, passersby could probably hear me, but I didn't care. We wept for all that had been lost. Only God could help us now. Feeling weak and experiencing a little pain like I had earlier, I quieted myself as best I could, placing my hand on my lower back.

Tory placed her hand on my abdomen and pointed at a chair. "Sis, sit here."

Zora said nothing, but watched with careful concern in her eyes. Thank God, she still loved me enough to care. We sat speechless for a few minutes, and then I headed to the bathroom to make sure I hadn't started spotting again.

Zora stopped me in the process. "I'm not your judge, but I am your sister. You did something—"

Tory interrupted Zora. "Hold up, hold up now. Please don't open another door none of us need to walk through. It took a lot for Rain to share that."

"Well, she could have kept it to herself," Zora snapped. It seemed like she needed more time to digest all I'd said. But at the same time, it seemed like something else was going on.

Tory sucked her teeth. "What is your problem?"

"I can't…I mean my problem…I can't…"

"You can't what?" Tory huffed with a slight neck roll, a habit she had worked hard to eliminate once she realized how other people looked doing it. She tried again. "What is it?"

"I can't have any children," Zora whispered as her remaining tears gushed forth.

Whoa.

Quietness blanketed the room. Zora's words lingered as the attention shifted from my sin to her pain. She hardly ever cried, so I knew her heart was indeed broken by all of this. In Zora's quiet voice, her agony resonated. Barrenness was an injustice for someone who tried to live with integrity and do the right things. Tory and I surrounded Zora and held her, the three of us rocking back and forth until she was limp. I figured Tory was crying for reasons similar to mine, because of things we'd shared in recent years. We both had past woes and life-changing events only God could heal.

In between her sniffles, Zora said, "I'm sorry. I'm so sorry, Rain. I mean, I don't agree, but I had no right to attack you for something God has already forgiven."

We hugged and sniffled some more. If we cried anymore, the three of us would need IVs for dehydration.

I came up for air and apologized too. "I'm sorry, too, Zora. The shame…"

"Hush now," Tory ordered us, "But I need to know, were you seriously planning to do that again?"

Dang, Tory. She had to ask. Outright lying wasn't an option, not at this point. Omission? Um, maybe. But to answer her directly, I boldly confessed, "I thought about it, and yes, I made the appointment."

"Why?" Both sisters cried in sync.

"Because once you open the door to the devil, he will try you again and he almost had me again. Same situation. Same dilemma. Same people. But God…"

CHAPTER 6

"Come on, girls. Clean yourselves up and be beautiful." Tory parroted Aunt Cynthia's favorite line. If she saw us today, she wouldn't claim us. Aunt Cynthia was easier than Mama, but shared her same sentiments. You needed to always look your best, even in the worst situations. You at least had to look like you were winning. You never had to look like what you've been through.

Tory grabbed the box of tissues from the nightstand and handed several to Zora and me. "We look a hot mess."

My sisters and I shared a laugh as we dried our eyes.

A tap sounded at the hotel door.

"*Déjà vu*," we whispered amongst ourselves.

"Who could that be?" asked Zora.

"Pastor?" Tory asked, her voice hopeful.

"Malik?" I added, figuring anything was possible.

"You had me call them," Zora remembered.

"I didn't say call Pastor. I said call Malik," I clarified.

"And I added...'call Pastor.'" Zora tried to look innocent, but there was something else in her eyes.

"Great." I had to look both Pastor and Malik in their faces. I hadn't even talked to Malik yet about any of the drama I'd just shared.

"Y'all don't even know which one it is at the door," Tory scolded. "Let me go see."

"Wait..." Zora said as she picked up her purse from the desk.

"Nope," Tory quipped, "the Bible says 'Be ye also ready,' so hurry up and get ready."

I was going to have to talk to her later about being a 'Scripture thrower.'

We rushed into the bathroom to fix our red noses, apply lip-gloss, and brush our tousled hair. Not much could be done about our noses and swollen eyelids, but I quickly changed from my pajamas into jeans and a top.

Another knock, this time firmer and more persistent.

"Just a minute." Tory sounded tickled. She enjoyed seeing us scramble around like we were in high school. Then, it sounded like she was humming, *Here Comes the Bride*. "Y'all ready? I can't keep the man waiting forever."

Him who?

Tory proceeded to open the door. Voilà. There stood Zora's dream man, Pastor Christopher Dockery.

"Everything all right?" Pastor appeared disturbed, perhaps by the long wait outside in the hallway. I'm sure he didn't want his good deeds to be evil spoken of if a church gossip saw him hanging outside hotel rooms and what not. I couldn't blame him for that. You never knew who was a part of the spy committee these days.

Tory smiled and said, "Come on in, Pastor."

"Hey, Pastor," I chimed in, although Pastor was preoccupied with staring at Zora. This was good for me because I hadn't finished the community project yet, nor was I ready to reveal the source of my anguish. Coming home to help out with the Christmas project at Jefferson Lighthouse Church, often referred to as JLC, was the worst move I could have made right now, but I had made a commitment and intended to see it through.

Zora extended her hand toward Pastor Chris and said, "Thank you for coming."

Pastor Chris held Zora's hand a little longer than he should have and responded, "It's my pleasure."

Zora cleared her throat like she had something stuck in it and said, "I'm glad you could make it. Earlier, I wanted you to pray for my sisters and me, but I think we're okay now."

"No, we still need prayer." Tory piped up, then mumbled, "Seems like y'all may need some prayer yourselves." One plus one equaled two. Maybe Zora and Pastor Chris needed a refresher math class because together they clicked, but they weren't doing anything about it.

Pastor Chris finally averted his eyes from Zora and scanned Tory and I with spiritual eyes. It was the look all preachers get before they pray. Pastor said, "We can join in together right now, but before we get started, there's someone here to see you, Sister Rainey."

Before I could speak or object, Pastor entered the hallway and beckoned my visitor to come in. *It'd better not be...* I covered my mouth as the man I had avoided the past few weeks stood in the doorway and fastened his eyes on the person he called the love of his life—me.

No more hiding, no more ignoring his text messages and calls and no more lies. There was no place to run. I was overwhelmed.

CHAPTER 7

Like a candle needs a flame, there was no denying or getting around what I felt for Malik. I loved him. Outwardly, I looked like I should have spent three more minutes in the mirror. Inwardly, I pulled everything together and never broke his gaze.

What was he doing here…with Pastor Chris?

Pastor Chris said, "Please, hear him out."

"Okay. Well, let's all sit down." I ran my fingers through my hair, butchering the comb through I had given it before we opened the door.

"If it's alright, I'd like to talk to you alone." Malik surveyed the others before zooming back in on me. He could command a room, which was part of the reason I was with child now.

Thank God for deliverance and forgiveness. I must have been touched by the heavens because for once, I was not thinking about sex when I saw Malik. In fact, I was genuinely seeing him—like I did when we first met, back when we both were searching for someone and didn't even know it.

"This is my family." I nervously eyed my sisters, and then reverted my gaze back to Malik.

Malik never flinched. He was determined to see me in private. "This is between me and you, baby. There's something I need to know."

My attention shifted to Pastor Chris. Had he spilled our earlier conversation? Pastor perceived what my eyes were asking and shook his head. He mouthed, "Listen."

Not ten minutes ago, I had been delivered. I didn't trust myself to keep my emotions in check if the room cleared. But suddenly, I felt a peace only God can give.

"We'll go get some coffee," Zora offered as she gathered her things.

Pastor and even Tory followed. After Malik's request, I had lowered my eyes and they remained downcast.

As soon as the room cleared, Malik started toward me, then stopped. He resisted what seemed to be the impulse to embrace me like he normally did. He probably wasn't sure how that would go over. Instead, he put his hands into his pockets. I imagine being in a room with me was too close for comfort and clearly too much for him to hold back his affection. Still wrestling with his emotions, he pulled his hands back out, shifted his weight, then rubbed his hands over his head. Finally, he walked toward me. When he had closed the gap, he lifted my chin so he could look into my eyes. "Is it true?"

"What?" What question was he asking? About the abortion? Me leaving? The baby?

"Don't play dumb with me, Ray."

Malik was serious, but using a nickname of mine meant he was still feeling a little tender toward me.

"Tell me what's going on…because I saw it all."

"You're scaring me. What are you talking about, 'Lik?" I had gotten into trouble before from releasing information before I knew what the person was actually talking about. I had to be sure he and I were focused on the same issue.

Malik stood by the same windowsill where I had poured my heart out earlier. Only now, he squared off like we were about to enter a fighting ring.

"I don't get down with this kind of stuff, but I had a dream the other night. In my dream, you locked me out and went into another room that was dark. In my room—the one where I was locked in, I saw… I saw somethin' that looked like an image, a light. I lifted my arms crisscrossed to cover my eyes from the blinding rays. The light dimmed a little, but not before forcing me to my knees. Before I knelt, I looked over into the room you locked me out of and all I saw was dark, like dark images or somethin'."

I didn't even know my eyes had sprung another leak until I felt the dampness fall to my hands. Malik seemed strange and that frightened me. He had never talked like this before, but I knew exactly what he had experienced. I knew the darkness he spoke of because I had walked in it.

Malik grabbed my hands and pulled me close. "Baby, it made no sense for you to be in darkness while my room had light. Is it true I did this to you? I brought darkness to you?"

I swallowed hard, unable to speak.

He hesitated and continued, "That makes no sense to me, but I heard these words—*the time is now*—while the light was around me. I don't have a clue what that means. The only thing I could figure was for me to love you enough to let you go, because I don't want no mo' harm to come to you, baby. I'd rather part ways than mess up your life."

I was amazed. I had had a similar dream to the one Malik described and I couldn't help but be thankful for the mercy of God. For a while, I lived surrounded by darkness. I had felt death, and it claimed my baby.

"Say something, please. Am I right?" Malik captured my hands in his and held them.

"Malik, you saw me in a place of darkness I'd put myself in. I locked both you and God out of my life."

"What about the light? This thing is messing with my head."

"Could it be God calling you to Him?" I carefully questioned him.

"Um, yeah, I thought about that." His hands escaped mine.

"And?" I prodded.

"I've talked to the pastor about that. I'm working it out."

I offered a huge smile and quipped, "In the words of my little sister, alrighty then."

"There was something else in that dream I didn't quite get a hold of, but I will eventually."

"Whatever it was, God will show you, Malik." I offered my spiritual insight, still somewhat distracted by what I was holding inside.

I needed to tell him and the time was now. He had a right to hear the truth from me, not the church's two busy bodies that hung out at the club. A lot of damage could be done with just a bit of information. Mama used to say, "They only have a page and think they got the whole story." I cleared my throat and decided to tell Malik all of it. If knowing everything meant I would lose him, or that he would think of me as trifling as the church hypocrites, there was nothing I could do. I had to live with my selfish, destructive choices.

For the second time this evening, I unburdened my truth to someone I loved. To my dismay, my big, bad, drug dealer Malik cried like a little boy, stuttering. "My m-mama... almost did away with me."

I had no idea.

He dropped to his knees, and I got down on the floor with him. I knew he hated breaking down like that before me, but he trusted me. As I held him, he struggled to pull himself together. I knew he hated letting his guard down like that. I wondered if something else was going on.

"I'm sorry. I'm so sorry for what I did. Sorry I was about to take another one of our children's lives, all because of what church folks would think of me." I cleared my throat as he gained his composure and confessed. "I took your money." I put my hand up before he could interrupt and added, "But I still have it."

"Girl, you almost caused a brotha' to go to jail for murdering one of those dudes handling my money. I knew it had to be you. I'm glad I didn't pull the trigger on one of them."

Malik clenched his fists and released them slowly. He took a deep breath and blew it out. Then he cupped my cheek, the roughness of his calloused palm gentle against my skin. Our relationship had been through a lot, but he remained tender toward me. He pulled me into an embrace and lay my head on his chest. It was a peaceful moment.

Malik drew a long breath. "Sorry, I wasn't there for you. I'm sorry about it all...my life, and uh...how I chose to live it."

We met nearly three years ago at the church's summer outreach program. I chaired the event and registered people interested in knowing more about the church and its ministries. Before I could look up from my clipboard, Malik extended his hand and made it clear his only interest was me. There was an instant connection. He began showing up to all the church functions. I finally made a deal with him. We would go out on one date if he came to church one Sunday, for all the *right* reasons. Not for me, but for himself.

I could have told my sisters I was dating the biggest drug dealer in town, but I kept him a secret. I didn't want to hear their many cautions. Some say he's killed before, but in my heart, I knew the truth. I was in love with an illegal businessman, not a killer.

Malik wiped the corners of my eyes, and I did the same for him. There was a knock at the door. Pastor Chris and my sisters were calling it. Our time alone was over. Arms folded across my chest, I stared out the window at the snow-covered pines while he opened the door. Pastor Chris entered, followed by Zora and Tory carrying a tray with coffee and creamer. The delightful aroma filled my nostrils.

Pastor Chris voiced the same question he'd asked the first time he entered the room. "Everything all right?"

Malik came to my side. "Yeah, I think so." I nodded my head in agreement.

Pastor Chris cleared his throat, "Then let us pray God completes the work He has begun."

I wished Pastor could ask God to give me some answers for all the questions running through my mind. I had to uphold my commitment to JLC and the Christmas program, and I knew now with Malik and I back in contact he wouldn't leave my side too long. Was I ready to be seen with him? With all of the danger he was in, was he capable of changing? And, if he changed, how would he click with the church? Would he be miserable?

I released a sigh.

We all joined hands, knowing healing was available for the taking and Pastor prayed. I hoped Pastor would throw in an extra word of prayer for strength to deal with the heathens at JLC.

Fireworks would be popping at the community event. I could feel it. I wondered who would strike the first match?

CHAPTER 8

Two Weeks Later

I kept my mother's letter with me and read it almost daily. I wanted to absorb every word. God was mending hearts. Each of my sisters were finding their own ground to stand on, walking out their own journey with a new perspective. However, we had one more giant to slay: the gossips of Jefferson Lighthouse Church. The women, two in particular, would turn my life into a disaster if they could. Jealousy, not my falling into sin, drove them to want to embarrass me.

Church folks. Before I moved away, I held positions they wanted to hold. But they could have them. This Christmas program was my last project, one of the reasons I came back home. I mean, really? Foolishness like this wasted way too much energy. For me, dressing up the outside while neglecting the spirit was out of the question now. After everything God had redeemed me from, I could never go back to the part I *should* play. My secrets had held me captive for a long time. But no more. I remembered God's grace, which allowed me to have mercy on others.

I would always remember when…

Today was a new day for my family and me. Forgiveness had come. Even though I had a ways to go to forgive myself completely, I was determined to face the rest of my demons so I could get to the *true* church, those who wanted to do better, and dismiss the ones who were up to no good. I wouldn't be going alone. The Thomas sisters made that clear. We went with a plan.

We had worked hard on the finishing touches for the big community event. My family, knowing about my scare at the hotel, kept an eye on me. They didn't want me to overdo it, which I was known for doing. Going beyond was in my DNA.

Inviting all the surrounding businesses to join us, Pastor Chris had expanded the event onto the church grounds. The lavish grounds were fit for kings and queens. Festive Christmas colors, with hints of gold, decorated the fellowship hall. Each table centerpiece displayed words of hope, faith, and love. Each visitor was given a stone with an encouraging message. Every creative detail was designed to build up the community.

Pastor had been preaching a series on love and was looking for a great manifestation of that theme. The church had grown in number, and Pastor was trying to cultivate love in the congregation. However, the people seemed restless. Lately, they were more about other people's business than God's business—definitely *not* about love.

Pastor Chris entered the fellowship hall with Malik. Four of Malik's "street" partners were with him. They looked skeptical of the church setting. I wondered how long they'd stick around, but at least they had come out.

"I know this ain't the preacher man coming on time!" Trina, never one for using indoor voices, zeroed in on Pastor Chris. Everything about her sounded like a marching band—loud. Malik's old girlfriend didn't understand two letter words like "no" and "ex." "Who's all of this you bringing? Is this your attempt at a so-called outreach ministry?"

Trina was being extra as usual, with her two buddies standing behind her. As suspected, they were the hands feeding her updates. It didn't take a college course to figure anywhere Malik went, she wouldn't be far behind like he was her oxygen tank. The way she managed to track him down, you'd think Malik had a programmed chip installed.

Malik left the pastor's side, probably looking for me, and if I knew him like I thought, he was avoiding any friction with Trina. He had already told her there was nothing between them. His heart was with me. He couldn't see me behind the partition as I put goodie bags together for the attendees. I scooted within earshot, careful to make myself visible only to Malik. I did a quick wave at Malik and he made an arrow path in my direction. When he got close to me, he kissed my cheek like he always did when we were okay. I loved that endearing gesture of his.

"I've been thinking," Malik whispered in my ear.

"Oh yeah? About Trina over there mouthing off at the pastor about you?"

"You know I don't care nothin' about no Trina. I'm done with that," Malik waved his hand in Trina's direction. "There's something I want to talk to you about."

"Okay," I responded. "But what is she doing here?"

"She here because she's shady. Don't worry about that. Look, Rain, I know you believed me when I told you I was done with the woman since you and I patched things up. It was never serious. I told her I love you. *You.*" He pointed a finger at me. "I need to talk to you—"

I hushed Malik by placing my finger to my mouth. "I want you to love me for me, not because of the…" I glimpsed down at my tummy and looked back at him. He would say anything to keep our connection, but I wanted it for the right reasons. For both of us.

"You know better than that. I loved you way before I knew about the baby, but now I love you more." Malik said those words with a smile and I returned his sentiment. I knew he loved me, but still I wanted to hear it. No, I *needed* to hear it. Unfortunately, Trina's rough voice spoiled my mood the moment I heard her get indignant with the pastor.

Pastor Chris would not allow any guest at his church to be disrespected or put in danger, not if he could help it, but Trina had been known to cut up with weapons and all of that. She fought childish and dirty.

"Answer me, preacher," she shouted. "Is your outreach ministry getting common criminals to come to yo' church?"

"Yes, Sister Trina. We go out into the streets, door to door, to spread the Gospel."

Trina had worked her way over to the reverend, swinging her hips and blond ponytail in the same direction as she walked toward him. She invaded his personal space as close as if she were his special one. I would have laughed out loud if I weren't busy finishing the goody bags. No need to become the focal point of this event before my time. As soon as Trina saw me, I'd have to block a verbal punch.

"Thanks for inviting me and my family, Pastor, or is it *Reverend*?" She said with a cloying smile.

So fake.

"Pastor is fine, sister." Pastor Chris scratched his forehead. "I'm glad you could join us."

"You want to sit at our table?" Trina asked.

Because it took a moment for Pastor Chris to respond to her request, she snapped, "Oh see, now I get it. We not good enough to be sittin' down with the good ole reverend."

"No, sister, it's not like that." Pastor Chris nervously surveyed the fellowship hall, but it was too late to find an escape. The people seated at nearby tables had already turned around with wide eyes, clutching their sherbet punch.

Pastor needed a ram in the bush. It was time for us to stand by his side and be used by God to provide some mercy. I jabbed Malik in his rib. Trina obviously didn't take rejection well and she wasn't about to let Mr. Fine Reverend dismiss her, even if she was in the church.

"It's not like that? Save it or better yet, save yourself!" Trina barked like a wild dog.

"Calm down, sister. I need to greet everybody," Pastor explained.

Knowing she had the floor, Trina dropped her napkin. After she saw the pastor wasn't going to fall for her false daintiness, she knelt, probably to make sure all the other men were able to peep at her exposed cleavage. "Y'all preachers always got some meetings or something going on. I know all about your meetings, especially the one with your girl, Sista' Rainey Thomas."

This pushed every limit. I knew Trina had her spy committee watching my every move. Someone must have reported back to her that I had come in to see Pastor Chris.

"Did I hear my name?" I had more attitude in my tone than I preferred in the house of the Lord, but I had to stand up to this woman raking my name across the churchyard. Ice clinked in people's glasses as they continued to drink and watch Trina's showdown. She loved being the center of attention.

"Oh good, you've met Ms. Thomas?" the pastor responded, not realizing he was walking into a trap the enemy had set for me.

68

I came out of my hiding place. Tory and Zora took up their positions and Malik stood by them as I positioned myself next to the pastor.

"Yeah, I know her." Trina gawked my way, put her hand up to hush me, and then turned back to Pastor Chris.

I wondered why she didn't look at Malik.

"She used to call and come by my club all the time, gettin' on my nerves, looking for Malik." There was no stopping Trina now. Unbeknownst to Pastor Chris, she was already mad. Malik had just told her he loved me. Because she had lost another round to me, she would make sure the church family knew I was no saint.

"Your club?" Pastor scratched his head.

"Yeah, my club. She messin' around with my man!" When she spoke this time, Trina looked at Malik as if there were unfinished business between them.

"I called once." I stood my ground. "I didn't *come* to your club. I didn't have to. Why don't you stop fooling yourself and lying about me to make yourself look better?"

"Lying? Girl, that's your first name. You need to stop trying to trap my man."

I paused before I responded out of frustration. My eyes darted around the room and landed on the wrong person, Tory. That was like passing the baton in a relay race.

"N…O…" Tory said as she drew letters in the air in front of the woman before I could stop her. "He said *no*. I heard him tell you to your face."

"Trina, stop this nonsense. It's over, it's been over." Malik added.

Trina gawked at Malik and he returned her stare. If you ask me, their shared gaze held a little too long for my taste. They definitely had history and I didn't want to know the details.

"Look, Trina. I didn't steal Malik or do anything behind your back." I planted myself at the forefront of the pack and struggled to speak rationally with her. *I'm trying, Lord, but these people, Lord...*

"You don't need to explain nothin' to me with yo' pregnant self." Trina spat the words out so loud the effect was like a needle stuck on a vinyl record. As her words echoed through the building, what stopped me from having a déjà vu moment like I had at the hotel, were the tears welling up in *her* eyes. I understood her dilemma. Broken and hurt people break and hurt people.

Members of the church gasped their unbelief. Some who knew me whispered my name, repeating Trina's newsflash. "Not Rainey..." others were saying. I wanted to glare at them, but resisted in order to please God. I didn't respond. Whoever said to ignore your enemies must not have had one like this ratchet woman.

"I know all about what you seem determined to share, Trina." Pastor Chris tried his best to maintain a civilized conversation, but his forehead veins were evident. I sent up a prayer to God to help him with this woman.

"Oh yeah? What happened to you calling me 'sister?'" Trina rolled her neck and quickly wiped her eyes.

"We've wasted enough time. Let's do what we came to do." Zora cut her eyes at Trina and proceeded to the microphone.

Standing back and taking it all in, I saw the heathen gossips, Lena and Josephine. Both women looked delighted to have Trina standing on the mountaintop doing all the dirty work for them. The smirks on their faces sang, "We've got the victory."

Trina's tongue confessed my sins when she needed to worry about her own. What they all didn't know was there was something different on me this time. I kept my head up, hoping people could see my new stance and that my demeanor loudly said, "There is but one Judge." The no-judging stance wasn't an excuse to feel better about my sin like I had done in the past. It was to give me courage. I wouldn't fear any of them.

On cue, Zora and Tory led a single file line into the hall and gathered behind the podium. Pastor Chris knew exactly what was going on and smiled.

"There's been a change in the program," Zora announced into the microphone, beaming with pride. "Today's message will be from Rainey Thomas, my sister." Zora then took her place next to Pastor Chris. The chemistry between those two was so strong. It wouldn't be long before they realized God had made them for each other.

Lena and Josephine immediately marched over to Pastor demanding to know what was going on.

"Pastor, I can't believe you're going to allow this woman, full of all kinds of sins to preach to these people." Josephine declared.

Lena followed suit, "I will leave the church if you allow this."

I looked over at my pastor, but he wasn't moved. Josephine and Lena's actions were far more severe, because they were seasoned. However, their actions lately showed they were still immature.

I thought about what I would say to the crowd as thoughts of shame, embarrassment, and even unworthiness flooded my soul, reminding me of my mistakes.

Maybe, these women were right. Did I seriously have the audacity to stand before these people, *God's people*, and offer anything good? *Lord, I need you.*

CHAPTER 9

T his was the Christmas season, the season to celebrate the miracle of that special birth, the season to embrace and share love, to draw people with the love of Jesus Christ. Today was a new day for this church, as it was for me, and for those who wanted to build up and not tear down. People have to be who they are until they become who they are meant to be in Christ. That's the message I would bring.

Pastor could not allow the loveless kind of behavior of Trina, Lena, and Josephine. "If you leave the church," he said to Lena and Josephine, "God bless you. But if you stay, you will learn to walk in love. The hateful words you speak have crippled the church body and driven people away. This cannot go on any longer, *not* at Jefferson Lighthouse Church. If you can't comply with the Word of God, then as you go, let others come."

Pastor looked at the three women. These ladies were so unhappy. They found pleasure in other people's falls. His prayers were answered right before our eyes as the three sat down holding on to what little dignity they had left. Their choice to stay shocked us all, and we—at least I and maybe the pastor—would have to ask God for help and forgiveness rather than wishing they would leave.

All eyes returned to me as I looked at the audience. My voice echoed through the speakers. "Today's message is '*He sent His Son for me.*'" I adjusted the microphone so people could hear me better. "Let me begin by addressing what Trina said. It's true. I'm pregnant."

I stood still and waited for the murmuring to simmer down. "I was living a life that was all messed up and not pleasing to God. In fact, I'm still working it out. I kept secrets. I lied. Yes, I sinned, but God sent His Son for me. He sent Him for you, too. Jesus *is* love. Church, we have to love people through their trials. It doesn't matter who they are or what they've done, love will bring them to the Son."

And I didn't even plan for that to rhyme.

Responses of "Amen" and "Bless God" filled the air in the fellowship hall. Malik took his place next to me at the microphone. Trina stood up, snatched her snacks from the table, and exited the hall. Despite her "ghetto" actions, my heart went out to her. I made a personal commitment right then to pray for her salvation.

I saw Malik's eyes scan the people before he began. "I ain't no' preacher. The only reason I'm standin' up here right now is because of Rain. She chose to love me despite my occupation and sinful ways, as y'all call it. Nobody from the church—*this* church—ever showed me *that* kind of love. I didn't want to be 'round a bunch of hypocrites. At least I *knew* what I was. Church folks always rattle off the directions for you to drive to but never use the same streets themselves. I never thought I was betta than anyone, but the church folks all thought they were betta than me. What's that scripture? Something about we fell down and have fallen short of the glory?"

Laughter erupted from the congregation when somebody yelled from the back, "You better preach, boy!"

"What I'm saying is my baby, Rain, accepted me for who I was and that action caused me to consider God. Christmas never really meant much to me before, but today I know the true reason. I'll leave you with this thought." Looking at me, he said, "I met Mother Thomas. She followed me on the street one day. She smiled at me and never looked down on me. She said these words, 'Son, there's a betta way.'"

Malik paused and put the microphone down, but then he picked it up again and cleared his throat.

"I can tell you this. I brushed her words off at that moment, but over time that one statement stuck with me. I found out that even in yo' darkest midnight, Jesus will find a way for you to get out of any situation." Malik cleared his throat once more, "I'll turn the mic back over to the pastor."

Pastor Chris and Zora took their respective places to continue with the program. It was wonderful to watch them work together. They looked good, like they should be husband and wife. I felt in my spirit they would work it out if Zora let the man love her. I laughed inwardly at the thought.

Zora, in her take-charge way, stepped up to the mic and said, "They passed out stones at the door, but we all have stones that remind us how messed up we are. Where are your stones? Do you have one, two, or have you lost count? Look at your life. How many times have you lied, cheated, ran…?"

Zora scooted over as Pastor Chris smiled and took the microphone. "Will the volunteers come forward?" Each of the five people in line with Tory stepped forward. They shouted the words on the cards they held before resuming their place in line.

"Have you lied? Liar."

"Treated someone poorly? Abuser."

"Talked about anyone? Gossiper."

"Killed someone? Murderer."

"Sold death masked as a good time? Drug dealer."

"Cheated? Adulterer."

Pastor Chris surveyed the room as if daring someone, compelling someone to stand up. "Everybody has done something they're not proud of. What was called out might not be your thing, but whatever your thing *is,* you need God to help you overcome it." He continued, "Let him without sin cast the first stone."

The room stilled as the Spirit of God hovered. Tears rolled down the cheeks of people who were convicted. Only time would tell whether they applied today's lesson or allowed it to fade. If only a few really caught it, the effort put forth by so many would not be in vain.

Pastor's eyes glistened. He clearly felt what he was saying. "I say it again…let him who is without sin cast the first stone." I watched Pastor Chris survey the room again. This time for an assurance the message had been heard, he locked his right hand with Zora's and lifted their joined hands toward heaven and prayed a blessing over the people. Peace filled the place. I know because I received mine. Or maybe it was just my soul finally finding rest.

I had no doubt Malik had bumped into my mother before she died because she regularly walked around town and shared the Good News of the joy she had with random strangers. I knew in my heart that even in the midst of my sin, my mother would have loved me endlessly. She would have opened her arms wide to receive me back, just as God had. No, she wouldn't have been pleased with my ways, but her love would have healed me. I should have known that before now. Maybe I was looking for an excuse, but now I understood the boundaries Mama set up were to keep me safe, not suffocate me.

I had learned a profound lesson indeed.

CHAPTER 10

After enjoying a savory homestyle holiday meal, an assortment of desserts, youth festivities, and lighthearted conversation, peace lingered as the crowd dwindled. Only a few people remained seated, sipping their warm holiday beverages or coffee. It had been an amazing evening. My sisters and I still had a ways to go, but we were not where we were three weeks ago. God had done something remarkable within my family, and JLC and me. Something gigantic.

The cleaning crew cleared the trash and swept the floor, working around those who were still enjoying themselves. It was nice to see people actually take time to fellowship in a good atmosphere. Despite initially not wanting to be anywhere near the church, I'm glad I was able to take part in today's event. A few of the members had surprised me with comments like "God bless you," "Thank you for saying that" and "Be encouraged." Their words were refreshing and blessed me in a way I didn't expect. Of course, there will always be a few people who will unjustly scoff at you, but God in His goodness has given me the grace to smile through their ridicule. I pray I *never* become like them.

I sat for a minute before wrapping up the night. My sister Tory came over with two cups of hot chocolate and handed one to me. I welcomed it. We both slurped and sighed, which made us laugh out loud. When our laugher subsided, we sat in silence for a moment.

She turned her chair toward mine, scooted close, and leaned over. "*So*, how did you do it?" Tory asked with downcast eyes.

"*Oh,* you want to know…" I paused so she would look at me, "how I put that *fire* out?" I discerned where she was headed, but wanted her to come out and say it because it was on her heart to do the same as me—change. Calling out her temptation was the best thing to do because too many people skate around sex, *especially* in the church.

I decided to be candid with Tory because it's not always easy to talk about this issue. The only thing we ever heard was don't do it! Fornication *is* a sin, but what were we supposed to do with our hormones?

"*So*…do you *really* want to know?" I inquired in a light tone, although I was sure my eyes told a different story.

"Yeah, because how do you stop doing something you crave and enjoy?" Tory's expression was playful yet serious.

"I hear you. I thought I'd never be able to stop because I like sex too."

"Right!" Tory squealed like a little girl.

"But, what I didn't like was the aftermath of feeling guilty."

"Right," Tory dragged out the word in a depressed tone as her eyelashes fluttered. I knew her inward struggle all too well.

"Hey, hey now. You can do this." In an effort to make her smile, I joked, "I've only been delivered two minutes."

We both laughed, then I took her by the hand and got *real* real with her.

"Okay, we both know sex is good, but here's the trick that helped me." I stared at her as she tightened her grip on my hand to encourage us both. "As long as you set your mind on *how* your body feels, sex is where you're headed. When I replayed each kiss, every touch and how I responded… Come on, you know what I'm saying. *Then,* I wanted more."

She nodded rapidly and released my hand to express with her hands, "Okay, if my mind is locked on how I feel, my body responds, setting me up all over again."

That's about it.

I gave her a minute to think about what I said as she probably replayed her own scenarios.

Tory nodded slower this time, as if she were having an "a-ha" moment. "It's a cycle."

"That's it. And, the mind is strong and vivid and will take you places you don't want to be," I emphasized.

"With one thought…" Tory stood with the half empty cup of hot chocolate still in her hand, then abruptly sat back down. "Okay, but how did you change your mind? *You know. Stop thinking about him*?"

"I thought about something else," I responded matter-of-factly and took one last slurp of my hot chocolate.

"Lies! It's not that simple. I tried that and it don't work," Tory snapped sarcastically.

I kept quiet because I understood her frustration.

Tory shook her head and folded her arms before saying, "I thought you—*ugh*—do you know how many times I tried to *not* have sex?"

"What? And I didn't!" I got adamant with my response. "It is a process, Tory. If you want to stop, you have to do the work. When I was in that hotel room, I repeatedly replayed my nights and mornings with Malik. I was ready to light the candles, call him up…something. But when the phone rang or somebody knocked at the door, it interrupted my train of thought. *See. So*, when the thoughts come, and they will—"

"You switch gears before you get stuck." Tory interjected with excitement.

"Yes, break the thought. Say something. Don't let the thoughts travel to the designated spot. Stop the traffic before it moves."

I allowed those words to settle. I lowered my voice as people neared the exit door by our table. "Look, sis. I came to a place where I had to put it *all* out there for God to help me. Getting attached was a danger zone for me. One touch struck my fire and the flames grew from there. You know what I'm saying?"

Tory laughed and nodded her head.

"Seriously though, if I were a fireman, I could never put out any fires. That's evident," I chuckled and touched my belly,

"But knowing the truth, *my truth*, I had to ask myself whether I wanted to die here. And the answer was, I didn't. It was time to change my mind with redirection. It wasn't easy, but I learned I had more power than I thought—one day at a time with God."

"Hold up. Wait-a-minute." Tory put her hand up like she was directing traffic. "You mean you told God *everything*?"

"All. Of. It." I leaned in close and said, "He's not surprised."

I sat back and smiled at my sister.

Tory seemed satisfied. She had a tool to help her get started on her new journey of abstinence. It wouldn't be easy some days, but it'd be worth it. We hugged in relief. This was a major breakthrough. I didn't see it that way at first, but I guess it was.

"Thank you, Rain. I love you, girl." Tory's tone was hopeful.

"Now don't forget—"

"I know. Don't set the night up to end in the bed or on the couch lighting candles," Tory summarized our conversation.

"And what else?" God had given us this moment. It was crucial to question her now that she wanted help. We would do this together and be a safe place for one another. I needed the accountability. Having my sister to pray with was an added bonus. Our supporting each other would strengthen us.

Thank you, Lord. You're still looking out for me.

Tory smiled as she answered, "I know my triggers, *and* God got me."

"If you let Him," we said in unison. With a giggle, I gave her a quick thumbs-up and added, "Because talking is one thing; doing is another."

We stood to help the cleaning crew tidy up. They had been more than patient with everyone. As Zora and Pastor Chris took down a few of the decorations, it blessed me to see Zora's steel wall down long enough for the man to make her smile. I was ear hustling and heard them talking. Their conversation seemed to flow without effort. They already had a coffee date set up. Tory and I planned to spy on them once we found out where they were meeting. Zora deserved to be loved by a man like Pastor Chris. I hope she kept the door open. Tender love was precious and seeing Zora smile was real good.

As for Malik and me, tonight was enlightening in spite of everything. It confirmed he was a good man. Because of Malik's height and unique swagger, I could probably spot him in any crowd. On cue, he made his way toward me with a warm smile and wide open arms.

I met him halfway. I needed a hug. *Mmmhmmm.* Malik's arms felt good and strong wrapped around me. I put into practice what Tory and I had just talked about and broke our embrace. *Lord, help me.*

We walked over to the back storage room and my heart raced a bit. I didn't know why I was nervous. When we got to an isolated spot, Malik placed his hands on my arms and positioned me in front of him. His eyes scaled me up and down. I was being tried.

I quickly averted my eyes, as my heart tried to skip. That seductive look of his had taken me there too many times. I was determined to slow the pace of our encounter. *No going back.*

"I've been trying to talk to you all night, sweetheart. There's something I need to ask you."

When a man gets down on one knee, a woman tends to think one thing. I don't know why women automatically go there, but most of us do. It was a huge deal for a woman who was anticipating that treasured question. For those who weren't, it could be a vexation. I couldn't say for sure what Malik was going to do, but if he asked, I was ready—or maybe not. Thankfully, I didn't have to find out because he was just tying his gym shoe.

"What I said out there was the truth, you know." Malik took my hand and pulled me closer. Before I knew it, I had released his hand. Holding hands would cloud my judgment. I needed to think clearly and focus on what I was hearing.

"You believe what I was saying? I spoke some truth tonight." Malik pulled me from my thoughts by swinging my hand, which he had grabbed once again.

"I know." I cast my eyes downward to avoid seeing Malik peer through me like only he could. It wasn't sexual. This was an emotional soul tie.

"Do you, because you looked shocked, or was that just amazement that I was out there talkin' to the people?"

Ahhh. Malik wanted validation.

"So much has taken place these past few weeks. Tonight was indescribable. I'm just excited about so many things." Of course, my heart was on God. But I tapped my stomach, reminding us both of the little one growing inside.

"Well, answer me this one question. Do you believe I'm a new man?"

I ran a quick word search through my brain to select the appropriate words, and then said, "Yeah."

I know it wasn't much, but it was all I could muster. I mean we were in the church. I wasn't going to lie or try to match the moment with watery words. The truth was Malik had changed tremendously and I loved him—*real* love and not mere lust. My flesh no longer sang his song on continuous replay.

We owed one another honesty. He had changed, but he still was Malik. Did I see him as a good father? Check. Did I see his potential as a good husband? Check. Did he love me? Without a doubt, but he hadn't *changed*-changed, if that made sense. His talk was right, but his phone calls were speaking another language. He was still in the game of drugs. Even, if I didn't want to believe it, I could *feel* it.

"Yeah? *Yeah?* That's yo' response? Didn't you hear what I said to the church people? To you?"

"I heard you. We all heard you, but did *you* hear yourself? Were those words for us, but not for you?"

Malik bowed his head, and then looked up sharply at me. He dropped my hand and started pacing as if he were angry. I held his gaze to see where he was headed, but he softened his brow and said, "I want us to be happy and live full lives with the baby in our new house—"

I cut him off, "I want us both to be happy and live full lives too. It just might not be…together."

"What? After all we done been through, you gon' stand up here and say we done?" Malik unclenched his fist, becoming animated. "We need to be married. I can do it right now." He pulled a black jewelry box out of his pants pocket and held it up to me. *"Bam."*

We'd never talked about rings or anything. I was surprised. I'm sure the expression was written all over my face. But at the same time, in my heart, I knew.

Even though we had never talked seriously about marriage, he obviously had thought about it enough to show me he was serious. It wasn't necessary for me to see the ring, and I didn't want to see it. Right now, I wanted my words to penetrate to his soul.

"'Lik, listen. Listen to me," I said. He stopped pacing long enough to take my outstretched hand. "You're different, but you're not saved. You know what kind of church person you don't want to be, but you haven't made a move to become the one you want to be either."

"This about the church?"

"No, it's about God." I received a blank stare after that bullet, but I couldn't stop now. I wasn't trying to go all deep and churchy on him because I understood. I'd just been there. Different issues, same situation. It was about giving it up. So, I fired again. "Are you still connecting and selling drugs?"

He rubbed the back of his head, quiet. He wouldn't look at me, and after a few minutes, he put his head down. I knew he had his own closet to work on and just because I was tossing out my old stuff didn't mean he was ready to bag up his. I gathered my jacket and purse, and placed my hand on his back as I stood by him and whispered, "I love you."

Malik grabbed my arm and turned me toward him. "Don't do this, baby. I thought you wanted to marry me."

I had never been one of those women who received her identity from a man. I didn't judge those women, but that just wasn't me. I'd seen too many of my girlfriends torn and broken up because they didn't have a man in their life. For me, marriage was the ultimate relationship. It wasn't the idea of being married that captured me because I still would have to live it out. There had to be something there—and we had that something—but we needed the glue that would stick between us. We needed the cross, not two seats together at church.

"Sweetheart, I *do* want to marry you, but I won't say yes…not right now."

I felt like I was singlehandedly destroying the bridge between Malik and God I had been used to help build. It took a lot for me to walk away from the man I loved while carrying his child. Both Malik and I would care for our child—of that I was sure. But, it was imperative we parted or I would compromise my beliefs. If that were the case, we only had a fifty-fifty shot, at best, at our marriage working.

Malik pressed his lips together and fought his emotions, but I saw the moisture filling his eyes.

I released the tears forming in mine.

"We both need to put some things into perspective. Maybe a little time apart will help us do that." He paused, as if in reflection. "Maybe after the baby, but not now."

I accepted Malik's full embrace. Today, standing before the church had been a huge step for him. But tonight, he'd be right back to his deals and I'd be waiting for a call I didn't want to receive. I didn't like the fact his preferred language was "hood" over the intelligent man with a business degree he was. I knew he talked "hood" to operate in the streets. In fact, it was crucial. My thing was, with a mind like his, he didn't *have* to hustle any longer. As long as he was into that kind of life, no way could I become Mrs. Malik Johnson. Easy money always has a price, making everyone involved pay the cost.

I'd just gotten back to saying, "Good morning" and "Good night" to my Lord, and I wanted that more. Everything else in my life would find its rightful place. No more skirting around the truth to fit things in. I loved me some Malik Johnson, but I would now embrace and hold on to my God.

I placed my hand on Malik's face and said, "I can't say yes to you until I become a queen who is fit for a king." I felt God's presence when I said those affirming words. *Never before would I have called myself a queen.*

As I tried to waltz by Malik without breaking down, he had to have the last word. He kissed my cheek and I kissed his. He whispered, "I hear you, Ms. Rainey Thomas and I'm coming to get you when I become the man you deserve."

With my back to him, I smiled as I walked away. As long as I stayed open before the King, He would let me know who my king and my future better half would be.

When the time was right.

In God's time.

The End

ABOUT THE AUTHOR

Known for dealing with controversial topics within the church community, Sonya Visor is an author, an inspirational "keep-it-real" speaker, a playwright and the founder of TruU Ministries, which was birthed from her inspirational book, Who I've Become. Sonya writes and ministers to help people become the true person God ordained them to be. Helping people unmask to reveal their true self is not only Sonya's passion but also the mantle of deliverance she lives and walks in.

When Sonya is not busy writing or ministering, she enjoys spending time with her better half, reading, watching a great movie and baking chocolate chip cookies.

Sonya resides in Wisconsin with her husband of over twenty-five years, Pastor Tony, and their two sons. Sonya and her husband pastor New Covenant Church, Racine.

Readers can connect with Sonya online and join the Unapologetically TruU FaceBook Community:

Sonyavisor.com | Facebook.com/sonya.visor |
Twitter.com/sonyavisor |

•Pinterest.com/unmask1• Goodreads

Sonya at sonya@sonyavisor.com and find more books by visiting her website at www.sonyavisor.com

Chapter One
INTERRUPTED—HOW I BECAME

"Are you having sex?"
"Uh…no, Mama. I'm not having any sex," I said, darting my eyes from my mother's gaze as I fidgeted with my school bag.
"I keep washing your underclothes, and I do not like what I'm seeing, Sonya. It looks to me like you are out there having sex with somebody!"

My mother was demanding an immediate answer. Here was my gate, my huge opportunity, to get this heavy burden off my shoulders. But I was scared. How could I explain all the wetness and discharge in my panties at age eleven? After years of being touched, fondled, and squeezed, my body was now responding to the very thing I hated—the touch of his hands. And I sure couldn't tell my mother that it was people we called … *family.*

As my mother's voice escalated, I'm sure the neighbors received an earful. "Sonya, you bet not be standing up here in this house lying to me!"

My mother stood there fuming while I remained quiet. I wanted to speak. But, the words… The words I needed to say should never pass the lips of an eleven-year-old girl. The words I needed to say screamed in my head then lingered on the tip of my tongue as I stood there with my eyes averted, feigning interest in the brown shag carpet that covered our living room floor. The words I needed to say stopped lingering and formed one solitary thought: *You should know who's touching me.*

I couldn't talk like that. Not to my mom. I was raised in the old school way that commanded respect to elders, especially your mother, and that would not allow me to disrespect her. My emotional frailty had nothing to do with her. So, there I stood impassive, as if I were a statue, trying not to move or blink to keep my tears from flowing. *This is our secret,* he would say…every time he touched me, every time he took from me. For five years, I kept his secret.

I couldn't tell a soul, not even my mom.

> "I tell you what! I'm making an appointment to take you to the doctor. Then we'll know."

I could have worked the streets as a prostitute at nine years old if it were left up to the hands that touched my body and changed my life. When most little girls were jumping rope, playing with dolls, or learning to braid hair, trusted family members abused me. Yes, several family members took advantage of the trust that comes with blood relation. My mother and father entrusted their most precious gift from God, their little girl, to family members who only saw value in my passive personality and femininity.

A man, who had to be in his late forties, introduced me to things no child should ever have to experience. And, my uncles perpetuated the torment. They were people who were supposed to love and protect me. Instead, they touched and fondled me. They taught me how to lie.

I should have told my mother the truth that day. Unfortunately, those same hands that explored my body served as an invisible muzzle. Their lies and perversion silenced and imprisoned me, creating cracks in the secure foundation poured by a mother and father who had a pure love for me. The abuse caused me to distrust my mother's ability to feel my pain and protect me. I believed the lies of my abusers and feared their wrath.

Threatened with the penalty of poor treatment, I kept my mouth shut and my head down. Standing before my mom, I transformed into someone I didn't like. I put on a mask. Inside I was far from the loving, caring, truth-telling, strong daughter my parents raised. I became something less. A perfectionist at wearing a mask.

I tried to be perfect. I couldn't allow anyone to see the pain, hurt, and confusion resting on me at the hands of my respected, beloved family members.

Trouble and shame pursued me. The transgressions of those who violated my life created scars that bled over and over again with each new incident. What was there about me that allowed them to mistreat me? I wanted to know what drew these people to me. What gave them a right to touch me? When they put their hands on me, they changed my thinking and awakened my womanhood well before its time.

With my innocence tainted, my outlook on life changed. The wide-eyed fervor and excitement of childhood I once had no longer existed. How could I climb onto my mother's lap and tell her what happened to me? How could I accept my father's protective embrace only to whisper my hurts into his ear? I couldn't do it. So, I covered it up and wore the victim's garment of shame. I became a superb liar. I learned to hide the wrongdoings of my abusers even though I hadn't done anything wrong…